Gander's Pond

For Stephen Fry
J.D.

For Ben, who likes rain
H.C.

First published 1999 by Walker Books Ltd
87 Vauxhall Walk, London SE11 5HJ

10 9 8 7 6 5 4 3 2 1

Text © 1999 Joyce Dunbar
Illustrations © 1999 Helen Craig

The right of Joyce Dunbar and Helen Craig to be identified
as author and illustrator respectively of this work has been
asserted by them in accordance with the Copyright,
Designs and Patents Act 1988.

This book has been typeset in AT Arta Medium

Printed in Hong Kong

British Library Cataloguing in Publication Data
A catalogue record for this book is
available from the British Library.

ISBN 0-7445-6704-1

Gander's
Pond

Joyce Dunbar

illustrated by
Helen Craig

WALKER BOOKS
AND SUBSIDIARIES
LONDON · BOSTON · SYDNEY

The sun was shining.

The day was very dry.

Panda was very thirsty.

Gander was very hot.

"I would like a long, cool drink,"
said Panda.

"And I would like a pond,"
said Gander.

"I shall make myself a long,
cool drink," said Panda.

"And I shall make myself a pond,"
said Gander.

"How will you do that?"

asked Panda.

"I shall wait for it to rain,"

said Gander.

So Panda got himself a long,

cool drink.

Gander waited for it to rain.

He waited …

and waited …

and waited …

until a cloud

appeared
in the sky.

Big blobs of rain began to fall.

"Now I can make a pond,"

said Gander.

Gander picked up a bucket and

stood in the yard, catching the big

blobs of rain.

"That will take a long time to make

a pond," said Panda.

"You need to run to catch the
rain faster."

"So I do," said Gander.

Gander ran around the yard
with his bucket, catching the
big blobs of rain.

But the bucket didn't fill any
faster.

"You need to run faster," said Panda.

"And you need a bigger bucket."

"So I do," said Gander.

Gander picked up a bigger bucket
and ran faster around the yard,
catching the big blobs of rain.

But the bigger bucket didn't fill
any faster.

There wasn't nearly enough
for a pond.
"You need a bowl as well,"
said Panda.
"Then you will catch enough
for a pond."
So Gander ran around the yard as
fast as he could with the bigger
bucket and a bowl as well.

Panda ran around with the
small bucket. But there still
wasn't enough for a pond.
"Perhaps if we try to catch it
in a tub, then we will have
enough for a pond," said Panda.
"You will have to help me,"
said Gander.

So Panda held one handle on the tub while Gander held another. They caught lots of big blobs of rain. But there still wasn't enough for a pond.

"I have an idea," said Panda.

"Why don't we put all our buckets and

bowls out with the tub to

catch the rain?"

"That's a good idea," said Gander.

So they put all their buckets and

bowls out with the tub to

catch the rain.

But the rain slowed down
to a drizzle.
"Oh dear, " said Gander.
"We need to put out all our pots and
pans and buckets and bowls and the
tub. Then we might have enough
for a pond," said Panda.

"That's a good idea," said Gander.

And they put out all their pots

and pans with their buckets and

bowls and the tub, but the rain

stopped altogether.

"I give up," said Panda.

"So do I," said Gander.

"Let's have a biscuit instead,"

said Panda.

So Panda and Gander each ate

a biscuit instead.

While they were eating

their biscuits, big blobs of

rain began to fall again.

They got bigger and ...

bigger and bigger!

They fell faster and ...

faster and faster!

Suddenly the rain stopped again.

"Look, the buckets are full,"

said Panda.

"So are the bowls," said Gander.

"So are the pots and pans,"

said Panda.

"But the tub isn't full," said Gander.

"If we pour all the water together,

we will have enough for a pond."

So they poured all the water

into the tub.

"Rub a dub dub, a pond in a tub!"

said Gander.

Then Panda had another long, cool drink while Gander made a great big splash!